Sugar Mountain

and the Descendants of a Man and a Woman Who Died Building a Wall

Sugar Mountain

and the Descendants of a Man and a Woman Who Died Building a Wall

Yong Hon Loon

杨 汉 伦

PARTRIDGE

To order additional copies of this book, contact
Toll Free 800 101 2657 (Singapore)
Toll Free 1 800 81 7340 (Malaysia)
orders.singapore@partridgepublishing.com

www.partridgepublishing.com/singapore

In memory of my grandparents and parents to whom I owe this.

1

When I woke I thought I was in the land of Sugar Mountain, but I was not. Then I realized it was not a dream; there were past lives to account for. Thus I realized where I was, and where I am. From it, I had awoken.

—An old reminiscence

I never met my grandfather. I did not really know who he was, what he was like, how he spoke, or where he came from. But I did have a grandmother, who saw his eyes in me. Through her, I had his name. She never left me, and she told me what he was like, how he spoke, and where he came from. When she spoke, I could hear the two of them talking. I could see the red azalea she wore in her hair on those warm summer nights. Everything he carried, and all that he left with her, for a long time without him, passed unbroken to me.

I was born with no known relation in the world, except for Grandmother. She cared for me after my parents died, and I came to live with her not long after I was born. We lived in dire poverty because of the war. Through Grandmother, who was around, and Grandfather, who was not, I knew there was a vast land filled with people who had a living, or waking, dream of a place called Sugar Mountain. Many dreamt about it, wished it, saw it, lived it, and still remembered it. For me, Sugar Mountain was a place I always carried with me. I had it with me, it lived in me, and it would not go away. From Grandmother and Grandfather, the dreams formed of what I was to become, what I became, and what I came to keep – after she died but never left me.

Whenever I heard her speak, I was carried across the realms of living minds. As I watched her thin, curled, and easily parted lips move, I heard in her gentle voice all I needed to hear. In her voice, I could imagine the sound of Grandfather's missing voice, something I never heard and would never hear. In my dreams, I saw a vast land, a people, a becoming, a wall, a living, a cause. These images did not fade; they stayed in my dreams. Through Grandmother's voice, everything I found, held, or saw in my dreams stayed with me in my waking hours.

It is an undeniable fact that we do not choose those who precede us, our ancestors. Rather, they choose us – a truth we always need to remember. We should remind ourselves that they once existed, and we exist now. And without them, we would not be.

2

Grandmother had a chest of fine, lacquered camphor wood, which she shared with her husband. When they parted, she took it from Grandfather and brought it across boundless, unforgiving oceans. The high-relief carvings, made by Grandfather, were of the same mulberry trees under which he and Grandmother first met. The design also featured the willows by the lake; a leak-plugged, flat-bottom boat moored near the bank; softly lapping waters; and swaying water lilies with pink, shy, half-open buds. This was where they spent their spring morning together, only to leave when the mist cleared. I grew up with scent of camphor; to me, it was and always will be the scent of my grandmother, who was around, and of my grandfather, who never was. In all the years I remember, Grandmother never locked the oversized, polished-brass latch. She did this to keep what was Grandfather's open and always close to her.

The best times to spend with Grandmother were next to that chest as she hummed the simple village songs, remembering the times of morning dew, of their childhoods. She never failed to open it on three occasions: Grandfather's birthday and the anniversaries of the surprise of the spring morning she met him, and the summer morning she opened to him. Grandmother, who gave me Grandfather's eyes, never had a tear in her eyes, which were deep and kind, not fully black or brown. When she spoke of him, those eyes beamed with the same joys of those special days that had passed and were hers. Each time she opened the chest, she would take out the items stored within that meant everything to Grandfather. She did this to look at them, as she had done many times before, as long as I remembered. Every time the chest was opened, the scent of the old camphor tree from which it came burst forth. The scent was a fragile, precious thread, connecting her to some distant past. It was a living link that stretched out, reaching further still to some yet unknown future, and with it came Grandmother's familiar closeness and warmth, and the scent of ink and paper from inside the chest.

Grandmother would drink heated home-brewed rice wine with her meal of rice, leeks, and eggs. For her, the dark, preserved hen's eggs were her joy in our dire poverty; for Grandfather, his favourite salted duck's eggs. To prepare the eggs, she would always wash them, being careful to keep part of the soil mixed with rice husks that covered the shells. The soil to her was a memory of times spent reclined on yellow hills far from their villages. As they relaxed, they would slowly drink the rice wine that was hidden and warmed by her breasts and his thighs in turn. Together they watched the stars turn and slowly dim as dawn approached. When she leaned over and fell asleep on a child, her only

grandson – the only relation she had in the world – the blush
of the rice wine on her high, smooth cheeks reminded her
of times on those distant hills, under the night sky where
Grandfather now was. As I looked at her, I would hear her
talk, but she was not talking to me. She spoke to him of
the many mornings they spent together. I saw the spray
from the river's edge glisten the ends of her dark hair, and
her wet lips opened wide in joy at the sight of red azaleas,
to close in the oblivion of endless dreams. On the summer
morning she called out again and again to Grandfather, as
her long legs stepped out into the morning air. The dew on
the grass breached her embroidered shoes to seek her virgin
feet turning red in the blush of the rays of first sunlight.

3

Allow these shaking fingers to make the finest woodblock prints of you, only in your crimson blouse, reclining behind the trellis of sleepy purple morning glories; only do not let the ageless, peeping pines nudge themselves too close to you in the wind – to forever take you away from these gnarled hands longing to hold you under your clinging thin tunic.

—An old reminiscence

One day when I was starting to understand, to speak, and to write, Grandmother opened the chest in the middle of the afternoon. This was an unusual time for her to do so. In a softer – or was it sadder? – voice (I regret not remembering) she made me look from her deep, kind eyes into Grandfather's and promise to look after what was in the chest. I was to do this for Grandfather and for her, but I was never to take out the contents until I was ready. There was a faltering in her voice when she repeated Grandfather's name, which was also a calling to me as long as she had me. With her sad eyes locked on it, she took out a letter, spoke Grandfather's name and then mine, and then softly murmured, 'I promise' as she wrote the date on it with her thin, fine, and delicate brush strokes. I did not realize it then, but this was the anniversary of the day she first said 'I promise' to him. It was the day she was betrothed to Grandfather so many years ago. She looked intently only at the letter, not my eyes, which were searching for hers. She looked for Grandfather, for the first and only time, and not from my eyes. In that moment, for the first and only time, I missed her. After that, I would never leave her again.

And many years later, at an age when I thought I was ready, I opened the camphor wood chest that Grandmother never saw reason to lock when with me. I saw the letter again, as pure, white, and fresh as when she had put it in. It was folded and held by the crimson hairpin she always wore. In it, rolled and bound with a single red silk ribbon was a short, sweet lock of curly hairs, pledged from both of them from their summer morning together. She had tied them together and kept the bundle inside a knotted yellow handkerchief embroidered by her with her name and Grandfather's name. There was the note she had left for me. In her brush strokes, which I would always remember, a memory lurked. I remembered her slender, long fingers – now old with age, but then, smooth and taut, with pure, thin, and transparent skin pulled over them, as she wrote:

(Grandfather's name which was mine), you are the same as (our name), whom I miss, and I know you will not open this chest until you think you are ready, many years after I am gone and with (our name). Remember, (our name), remember it all for me in opening this chest, as I know you will remember me. Let (our name) stay with me in you. By opening it, you will not have left (our name) and myself unfulfilled or unhappy. We waited, and you are now here for us. Treasure all the things in this chest as I have treasured them, without and for (our name). Then destroy them. I could not tell you then, but now when I am no longer with you, you will understand. Remember, (Grandmother's maiden name as she would have written to Grandfather) is fulfilled and happy that this happens today.

(Our name), when I was with you, at that time of year, I did not see the azaleas in bloom. Neither did I see the peonies, or the plum blossoms. But, in the dream, this dream, which is our dream, I saw the bamboos now flowering together in that rare occasion after years in waiting; they are bursting through the frost in the bite of winter, before the promise, our promise, of spring. In (our name) I am in you and never left you.

Deep in the camphor wood chest, separated from other contents below by a slat of finely sanded camphor wood were colour and black-and-white woodblock prints, flattened by a wooden weight, kept in a pouch of fine sheepskin. And

under the midsection of the other contents, forming the
bulk of items in the chest, were the original woodblocks,
with the dried colour and black inks still on them from
when they were last used – only once – for printing by
Grandfather. These were all neatly arranged and stacked,
with red silk ribbons holding the sets together. Grandmother
had never untied them. When I untied them for the first
time since they had been packed and had come across the
wide, unforgiving oceans, I realized that Grandfather had
drawn Grandmother in all the woodblock prints.

4

Thus she lay, languid, longing, forever mine to hold, her head on embroidered cushions. No one could be compared with her – her ever-calling voice that I hear, and her pure, white breasts and thighs, and straight legs, which will always keep me awake in this dream I cannot wake from.

—An old reminiscence

With my limited knowledge of the art of woodblock, I saw in front of me a treasure trove of the finest pieces of woodblock prints along with the original woodblocks, all done in the rich tradition that developed as the craft transformed into a fine art form. Unlike the outside of the camphor wood chest onto which Grandfather had carved high reliefs of mulberry trees with lake-side willows and water lilies without human figures, Grandfather had, in the woodblock prints, produced images based on himself and Grandmother. They had been drawn to each other, had searched for each other, found what they wanted in each other, and did not, and would never, let each other go. There was nothing between them, as they held each other, believed in each other, were consumed in each other, each taking the other to the joy of realization, of complete abandon and fulfilment. There was not just the summer morning – *their* summer morning – but spring and autumn mornings and nights, when it was never too cold for them to be outdoors, and winter evenings in bed by the light of an oil lamp. The scenes were in several series, dated, and divided by seasons or periods after they met, when they always sought, became renewed in each other, searched and then found ... over and over again.

Next to the scenes on the prints were side notes created in brush strokes by both of them explaining what had been drawn and printed. Each note reflected their devotion to each other. Together with Grandmother's fine, thin, and delicate brush strokes, which I had kept – and would always keep – in my memory from her letter, were Grandfather's bold, round, and soft strokes, which I saw then for the first time.

Grandfather had been a woodblock cutter, and then an engraver of books. He had lived and studied with an engraver family, and had done engravings in the distinct style of the period. But spread in front of me, the paper yellowed with time but the dyes still in pristine state, were all the unique colour and black-and-white prints of himself and Grandmother, printed only once, and at his creative height, and brought by Grandmother across the oceans from

Sugar Mountain and kept unseen by me till then, when it was for me to keep my promise.

And for the first time, I felt the same way Grandmother must have felt when she had to part with Grandfather, never to see him again. I could not bear to destroy any of the prints. They were of Grandmother and Grandfather, and were the only surviving part of them and the lives they had lived, shown to me alone. They were like the fragile end of the thread that connected them to me, the only one of us who was left, and who would not be without them. And, for the first time, I felt differently from the way Grandmother would have felt – that Grandfather, whose name was mine, would never forgive me for destroying his total devotion, even in his art, to her, and to her alone. And I should not have made my promise to Grandmother on the anniversary of her betrothal. But Grandmother knew me even then.

Not long after, the only promise to Grandmother I finally broke was to keep a single piece of woodblock of only mulberry trees and willows by the lake, which, together with her letter and the lock of hair bound in red silk ribbon, was all that remained of her and Grandfather, together with his name, whose voice, unlike Grandmother's, I would never ever hear across the wide, unforgiving oceans.

But Grandfather's and Grandmother's writings in their respective brush strokes I had reason and good sense to keep, to treasure, and then write from. The promise to Grandmother was never for them – until I had them also destroyed some years on, in their memory, on the day of the summer morning she opened to him, later with belated regret, as reminiscences drifted as endless, lapping waves, reaching far, unseen oceans, in old age.

5

Then I am surprised as I turn to look back. You stand near the willows under the mulberry trees, looking back at me out of a dream no longer a dream, a waking without awakening, a beginning, but not any beginning.

—An old reminiscence

For me, in all that Grandmother and Grandfather had left behind, and in what they wrote in their own way what others had written, I found lucidity, flow, connectedness, brevity, and yet depth, understanding, honesty, truthfulness, and their mutual conviction, which I could write from. They were always direct and incisive, never superfluous, always unpretentious and unassuming, enduring, with a total aversion to prevarication, all that was untrustworthy, twists, dishonesty, and superciliousness.

They were always written, with her hands in his, he on her, or she on him, with nothing between them. Or written individually by her or him, with the other always beside, nothing covering them. There were overlaps of brush strokes matching overlaps of words and phrases, points and counterpoints – after the surprise of the spring morning. They wrote, had each other, went to bed, wrote again, had each other again – with surprises, always fresh, in brush strokes in their writings, often with unexpected changes and smudges in between – all made, always warm, in and out, with their bodies close, in their total devotion to each other, in their immersion in themselves and in what they wrote – living, throbbing, flowing, unseparated, and inseparable.

And Grandfather wrote of beginnings very early on. It was the day after the surprise of the spring morning itself, after Grandmother herself started writing with him – the day when I also began to write.

According to him, it was lived, then said and heard, heard and told, and told and heard again. No, in truth and in fact, *it came about that …*

If it had not come about, nothing would or could have been known to have existed. Nothing would be written, and in that way, everything would or could be different. It might be told and heard, and then heard and told, but not in that way that had existed; or it might not have been told and heard at all. There would not be that, or even *a beginning* to Sugar Mountain – to what came about, had been, was, and what came after. Those who heard and told, those who then told, those who then heard, those who wanted to tell and make it heard were from – were *of* – Sugar Mountain, and they made it that the way it was. So, in actual fact, *it came about that …*

And only then, following what came about, what was lived, after it was told and heard, then heard and told, was there a beginning to the telling, to Sugar Mountain. It could be very different, as always happened; or it could no longer be lived, no longer had been lived; or it could, sooner or later, be destroyed, as always happened, or even forgotten, if enough were destroyed, or enough were killed, or time had passed it by, dead as silent, non-survival, standing monuments to what had lived before. But, for the land of Sugar Mountain, *it came about that …*

For the living, the telling and hearing, the hearing and then telling gave them an unbroken link, a fragile, precious, living thread to it, a true beginning to a vast land, a people, a wall, a living, a cause, a being – a dream that was not a dream.

6

No, never weep a tear for me for, with this quivering voice, what I have now to tell, what to whisper. The cold travelling wind of winter carrying it will bring me to you, to let these lips come to you, never ever to leave yours again.

—An old reminiscence

A group of all who were known to have the sharpest minds in the land of Sugar Mountain were rounded up, Grandfather wrote. They were rounded up as they always had been, on pain of having their heads cut off, to chronicle the times since the beginnings of Sugar Mountain when *it came about that …*

All were to meet their respective, expected ends, as always happened, except for one, who just sat very upright without blinking his eye, silent throughout until asked to tell his tale, and whose eyebrows and eyelashes, but not the hair on his head, were white, even whiter than the white fallen snow outside, but who was the solitary one whose head was spared, as if no one among them could ever be like him, to have a colour of hair different from that of his white eyebrows and eyelashes.

Grandfather, at this point, wrote with a nod to an old literary tradition in which there were no stops throughout the passage, and I wrote from what he wrote. The one with white eyebrows and eyelashes, but black hair, spoke to lengthen the time before his head would eventually be cut off, if it would be cut off. And throughout his account he would, here and there, without letting his would-be executioners notice too much, say something – a phrase here, and another there – that might lengthen a little the stay on the removal of his only head – only a little, just a little, which was all he could hope for.

The one whose head, for that moment, had been spared began his very long account, to which he owed his singular head. The people, he declared, were not, originally, sentient. It took a long time for them to stand upright, but they were still not yet sentient. So it was not easy, and it was never going to be easy. But already, from that early on, they were as bamboo that bent but did not break. So *it came about that ...*

The land was vast. They gathered, initially, in small numbers, isolated, huddled together because of the dark, the hunger, the anger of lightning, and the ever-merciless floods. To live, they shared fears. Standing upright, they had hands to reach out. They gathered together, so they had each other and not loneliness, which gave them their greatest fears. And they shared this connection with those who gathered.

Those who were not included were left to die, or were eaten by animals. Despite not being sentient, they could see what happened to those who were left out, and they feared being left out, without each other. They shared; they sought each other. This ameliorated their discomfort from the isolation, the dark, the hunger, the lightning, the anger of the vast land. Already, a long time after they started to stand upright, they had come to have a unique, common complexion – fair, slightly yellow skin found only in Sugar Mountain, which pleased the mothers very much when they looked at it in their naked babies. It moved the groins of the men when they saw it in the women's breasts and thighs in the morning, and when they saw them after their hunt, and again in firelight that relieved the dark, cold, and damp. And the women, in turn, heaved their breasts when, against their lighter skin, they saw the darker shades in their men, and in their groins.

Although their skin was fair and slightly yellow, some hair from their ancestors who preceded them remained on their heads, in their armpits, and in their groins. And it moved the groins of the men, who – having seen the breasts, thighs, and legs of the women no longer hidden by hair – also saw the common fair, slightly yellow skin contrasted against the hair in their groins and the hairs of their underarms, which had the same attraction. And the hair of the women attracted the men to the part of the women that they could impregnate. In turn, the women were attracted to the men who could impregnate them. Then, a very long time after they stood upright, long after they lost the hair on the rest of their bodies, and as they began to become sentient, they started to have anxiety that inspired them to cover themselves up, unlike animals.

To cover up – to keep and own their bodies, or another's – they used the skins of animals, which also kept them warm when they were without fire. So *it came about that …*

As they gathered, they covered themselves, and each other. Within the gatherings, despite gathering, or because of it, they began to fight, to kill each other. They did this because of hunger, because of the differences in the people in the gatherings and, among the men, because of their desire for the women who were now covered up, and because different women who had joined the gatherings moved their groins.

When they gathered, when they fought, when they desired different women, when they sought each other out, when they killed each other, the people could no longer be insensitive to each other. *It came about that …*

The men, because of their greater physical strength, which came from their ancestors who hunted and preceded them long before they were able to stand upright, and because they were the ones to impregnate the women, began, even as they were becoming sentient, or in spite of it, to possess, to subjugate, to own the women in the gatherings. And the killings were not just to ameliorate hunger, but to possess the women. And women, because they carried, gave birth to, and breastfed babies, had men who possessed and owned them, and fought for them, while the gatherings sought, as always, to ameliorate the isolation, cold, hunger, lightning, floods, and the anger of the vast land.

And those with greater strength, because they could, fought to own more women, whom they could impregnate even though they were covered up. And those who were more sentient – even women – could not always overcome physical strength; physical strength could still easily counter being sentient. So the killings continued when there was hunger, which was always there, and when men tried to possess women owned by others. *It came about that …*

As the land was vast, the people began to gather in different groups and locations, and many of them, as they became larger, began to be protected by men who, at any given time, were stronger, more threatening, and more dominant. They could also possess more women. But as these dominant men became weakened, sick, or old, others took over to maintain, to keep the gatherings, which ameliorated the chances of hunger and protected them from the threats of other gatherings, which always could become stronger. And the stronger the people, and the larger their number in their gatherings, the better they were at killing the people in other gatherings and at taking their food, animal skins, women, and other possessions. And, as they became more sentient, those who could gather and work together, and make weapons from stones, wood, and animal parts, grew in strength. Always vigilant that other gatherings did not grow greater in strength, they protected their land, women, food, and possessions. For, as the gatherings became larger, food became scarcer. Taking over other gatherings and killing their members solved that problem.

Weaker gatherings were wiped out; men died of starvation, and their women were carried away. As the land was vast, however, some small, isolated gatherings remained. They survived, especially because there were fewer men and women to feed to ward off hunger and starvation. And, in order for the larger and stronger gatherings to attempt to take over these small and isolated gatherings, they had to put their gatherings at risk, as the fighting men had to travel far distances and leave their own gathering unprotected. Thus *it came about that …*

As the food became scarce, the gatherings learnt to plant grains. In their legends, the seeds of a grass plant, as widespread as all grass plants in the land, as common as the people of the land, were accidentally spilt on soil in shallow ponds. They began to grow in season, providing more plants with seeds. This seed – rice – was cultivated and eaten by the people in Sugar Mountain; in fact, it became the staple food of the people there, who, in their large, sedentary numbers, had to be fed. And the cooked grain made for full stomachs when other food was scarce. Increasingly, where parts of the vast land were fertile, even with the seasonal floods, the rice came to be planted.

And as the people become more sentient, they domesticated animals and worked with tools to irrigate, to plant, and to harvest the rice, and to build granaries, just as they had built their dwellings. *It came about that …*

At this time, before the people had language, they were using sounds that came out of their mouths to express their joy, pain, sadness, excitement, loss, fear, warmth, surprise, approval, hatred, anger, aching, longings – and to voice desire, possession, and jealousy. But, as the people became more sentient, the beginnings of a single, common, spoken pre-language developed. It was used for simple understanding within the gatherings, and it worked. And the most-repeated utterances and words came to be used with nearby gatherings – even those who attacked. Some of the gatherings were attacked and taken over by stronger ones, with greater numbers and stronger weapons. The attackers took over land for planting rice, to fill granaries, to ameliorate hunger. They possessed the women. Therefore *it came about that …*

The women with fair, slightly yellow skin found only in Sugar Mountain since the time of their ancestors came onto their own and were desirable to the men who possessed, protected, and owned them. The men who saw them sought them as wives, to fulfil their desires and to bear their children, which was what women could do for those who possessed them. And as there were men who were strong or stronger, and whose possessions were more and plentiful, they could possess more of the women as they wished to fulfil their desires, to bear them even more children. For as they were strong, and had greater possessions, the women, who sought to be better protected and to own greater possessions, sought them. So it become the practice of the land, in their customs and rules, that each family was expected to have a single head – a man – right as a rooster among hens, and one or more wives, depending on how strong or capable he was as well as the wealth of his possessions. In taking many wives, the men, who agreed with the customs, did not lay down rules on number. So the men could take as many wives as they wanted, to ensure procreation and therefore their posterity. And, in becoming their wives, the women agreed to stay chaste to their men who could marry other women if they wished.

And those men who were stronger and owned more possessions arranged marriages among their children, even when the children were still young, to ensure the possessions were still kept among those who had them. But when the sons grew up, even though they were already betrothed to a particular woman, they could have more wives as they wished. And, as the practice worked, men were satisfied, and women continued to bear children. The custom became widespread and lasted for a very long time in Sugar Mountain, for it ensured more hands to plant, grow, and harvest the rice, to fill granaries, and to hunt for food. Thus *it came about that …*

Since the people had begun to speak it, the pre-language, the spoken language, had spread among people in ever-larger numbers. With their toils, difficult lives, needs, joys, and desires, they continued to express themselves to each other and beyond, to nearby, friendlier gatherings. They used the language to obtain food, to work the land, and to share. In time they extended its use beyond these daily needs. They used language for continuity, and their legacy, for names, dates, births, ceremonies, good harvests, occasions, burials, and festivities. And long before they began to write, they told and passed on stories, tales, imaginings, divinations about ghosts, dragons, and magic. These stories would outlive them and their gatherings. They were precursors of legends, tales, stories – histories by word of mouth. This set them apart from their forebears, who had left nothing of themselves behind. Thus *it came about that …*

The great rivers in Sugar Mountain, which flowed and moved like the dragons of the people's legends through the land – benign, unpredictable and merciless – killed many in their floods but also provided fertile land where the rice could be grown. And the people, who used the rivers to carry the rice throughout the land, lived and grew in greater numbers.

7

As he ran up the hills, he heard her laughter reach with the wind to the valleys below, through the pines, to echo in the mist rising in pure light through her velvet sleeves to the crimson curtain of floating dreams.

—An old reminiscence

Grandfather and Grandmother, who could be in bed together with nothing between them but a throbbing warmth, then paused in the telling of the long account of the one with white eyebrows and eyelashes, and hair black as burnt wood, and wrote an account of a boy and a girl who met at a time when there was no language.

He kept running up the yellow hills where there were no paths, Grandfather wrote. And, as he ran, his straw sandals left a shimmering, living, moving dust trail that, in the hot afternoon sun, slowly settled again on the warm, dry soil long after he left. But there was no stopping him. With the ever-close wind blowing into his face, his mind kept returning to the scent of her breath and the curve of her breasts, which moved as she giggled, and heaved with his touch. He remembered the laughter of joy that came from her – hidden, blushing, unfolding, calling for him. Her willingness, her presence, her desires, and the openness that emanated from her and never let go kept coming back to him, brushing him as if, in the wind, he was touched by her fine, curled hair. Then, as he tired near her village, he felt inside him the fervent glow unfolding that was within her, fragile, soft, keeping, yet wanting again, and yet again.

In her undisturbed world without language, of unheard murmurings and desires, Grandmother wrote, she saw him again in her dream, wished for, loyal, constant. And in this dream, she felt again the touch of his large, soft hands, a presence that was always there, in the earlier unknown, but then opened the world of her silence, where he could hear her, timidly at first, shivering, warm, belonging and possessing, wrapping him in a joy of cries, of yearning, flowing from within her.

And as he came to her, shy as a water lily with its pink, half-open bud, and she clung to him, she gave out a cry – shrill, soft, warm, urging, and seeking – in a tender call from her to him, of pure, unmade words.

8

And Grandfather and Grandmother then went on – in their own pre-language – to make phrases and sentences, strings of words consisting of sounds, written not for their meanings but for how close they were to the sounds they made in their devotion and desire for each other, with pauses here and there, highs and lows, and the range of tones in the language. The strings were broken into many parts, those in Grandfather's brush strokes, and those in Grandmother's. And in the two brush strokes, in the beginning, there were ever-present surprises and turns in which one would appear, then disappear, then meld into the other, mid-phrase, mid-line, and mid-passage, always with the overlaps of sounds chasing one another. Then, sometimes a string of brush strokes would be longer, while, at other times, the other would be longer. Eventually, the parts that were longer usually ended in higher tones – and they were normally Grandmother's brush strokes. There were many of these long ones in her brush strokes, with Grandfather's continuous, but short and intermittent, brush strokes in between, until one reached fulfilment in high pitches and tones. And often there were smudges mid-string, sometimes between strings, and at the end of strings. After these, there would follow the low tones in the calm strokes of Grandmother, no longer the tones of excitement.

Eventually it would be Grandfather's brush strokes, in the long parts, reaching an attainment of high tones in the end, matching Grandmother's high tones – of words without meaning. And they would be repeated, the short tones suddenly bursting through, until a long string of one ended in a high, followed not long later by the other.

They were tones of excitement, heat, warmth, joy, and sharing, full of meaning, but only in the sounds they made, which they shared only with each other. For, to Grandmother and Grandfather, where there was no language, the sounds of excitement, of warmth, and of joy were pure, unhidden, and full in themselves, without the need for words for their meanings to be understood. And only after they had found and fulfilled in each other that for which no words were needed, they would always end each episode in a return to language – to words with meaning meant for each other, a phrase or sentence in Grandmother's brush strokes, followed by one in Grandfather's.

And, in their excitement in each other, Grandfather would go on from there to immediately paint – without sounds made with words, but where no words with meaning were needed. He would paint Grandmother and himself on rice paper. His paintings reflected their joys of the very many settings they had experienced – indoors and out, in spring, summer, autumn, and winter, days and nights. He made both colour and monochrome paintings that he would later translate into woodblock prints.

9

Grandfather continued to write his story – the one with white eyebrows and eyelashes, but black hair, having said enough to stay the cutting off of his only head, up to this point, rolled his eyes, and, for the first time, turned to look timorously at his would-be executioners before he continued in a less-sombre voice.

Like everyone else, he continued, not entirely certain his would-be executioners were even listening, which was not a bad thing, he had an as-yet-unbroken bloodline to pairs of non-sentient and, later, sentient beings. Having no memory or remembrance of this did not mean no trace existed at all to the original pair, or to other pairs of beings somewhere or anywhere along the very long line that led to the present. It was just that a present-day mind could not see or find a connection without evidence, account, historical record, or anything handed down through time. That mind could not possibly reach the state of being that began a long time ago, but the link existed, whatever the current mind knew or saw, and it existed within the present-day being who owned the mind.

This mind might not be able to see, to understand, to deduce, but the link to its distant past, the reason for its existence today, could be attributed, depending on how far back the trace went, to a pair of sentient beings, or to an earlier insentient pair. But, whatever point of time the link was traced to, in the line of beings that led to the present-day mind, at each point of the trace, there was only a *pair*. The reason, the cause of existence, the coming to fruition, would be traced to this. Each original urge, either his or hers, or urges of both of them, led to the chain, down through the generations, of existences. The series of urges at different points, separate, unknown, unseen by the others, linked and led to each other, all subsequent urges not possible without the earlier, right down to the immediately preceding ones. And at each unique urge point there would be a cause, a reason, a relenting, an accident, the use of force, rape, passion, acceptance, compliance, unwillingness, consent, joy, hatred, passivity, concession, circumstances, surroundings that were unique to each pair. And each pair was the meeting, creation, willing, attainment, or ugliness, unhappiness, unacceptance, passivity – and culmination – that led to subsequent generational pairs who met, created, attained, were unhappy, did not accept, or were passive – and culminated – in their time. Whatever and whichever urge point was looked at, all of them were irreversible urges if unbroken – the attraction of another being, the desiring, willingness or unwillingness, skin, breasts, hips, hair, scent of breath, thighs, legs, feet, thrusts, flow – and a consciousness, to some degree or other, of existence, the

Yong Hon Loon
杨 汉 伦

meaning of being, of the present, of continuity, and the ultimate contribution of being. The chain was unbroken; the link remained. And the present being would search for another, an end of an urge chain to keep the unbroken link. The present being might not know or even understand it – as an end it had looked into the eyes of another unique end of ends that kept all links, future and downwards, *present*.

10

When the one with white eyebrows and eyelashes, but black hair, looked again at his would-be executioners, they, for the first time, seemed to look at him, for when he talked of pairs, they were uncertain if he was talking brazenly of the yet unbroken link, which was himself, or of all unbroken links. Already sitting upright, Grandfather wrote, he sat even more upright, as he had to show he knew what was expected of him, even though they did not say a word as he continued in a more sombre voice.

As they had rice to eat and their numbers grew, he continued, the people began to live in larger communities. And those who were stronger, more threatening, and more dominant not only owned and possessed more women but now possessed strong, threatening, and dominant men under them – pledged and loyal to them. This enabled them to oversee and rule the villages and entire communities. These men who had loyal ones beholden to them had land, rice-fields, and full granaries and possessions. They could leave it to others to till the land and take care of their possessions, giving them time to oversee, to take charge, to rule. For it was not enough that they had more land, rice fields, granaries, and possessions. Those with such wealth had to make sure that others who had less did not try to take what was theirs. They had to protect what they owned and ensure that their wealth was not stolen or destroyed. These strong, threatening, and dominant men who were loyal to them could provide protection, provided he kept them fed, even if they did not till the land and grow rice.

In time, as the communities grew larger, those who oversaw and ruled the communities, had larger numbers of men loyal to them. And these leaders might not even be the ones who owned the land, the rice fields, the granaries, and other possessions, for those who had large numbers loyal to them, but who owned nothing, could now, with the help of their large numbers loyal to them, take over the land, the rice fields, the granaries, and the possessions of those who had them. Or, if they could not easily obtain control of these, they could burn or threaten to burn them down. For those who were powerful saw that having strong, threatening, and dominant men under them meant becoming not just the ones to own land, rice fields, granaries, and possessions, but becoming the ones to own other men from whose land, rice fields, granaries, and possessions they could exact whatever they wanted to feed themselves and those who were loyal to them. Thus *it came about that* …

In the long history since the earliest times when the people had rice to eat and their numbers grew, wars and battles were fought, lost and won, won and lost, and lost and won again as the rulers eyed the communities and the land, which were eyed by others, and so it went on. And the people who had rice to eat and were greater in numbers conquered and killed, or were conquered and killed, in turn, in the ongoing turn of events in the land that came and went with the strength of the rulers and their forces, and the strengths of other rulers, whether singly or together, and their forces. So *it came about that* …

Just as very long ago, after they became upright and after they had fair, slightly yellow skin, when gatherings attacked, robbed, and killed each other and possessed the captured women, the rulers of large swathes of lands and communities attacked, robbed, killed, and possessed the captured women, only to be attacked, robbed, killed, and have their women possessed in turn.

11

Grandfather, who could be under the oil lamp with Grandmother with nothing between them but only their desire for each other, then paused in the continued telling of the long account by the one with the white eyebrows and eyelashes, but black hair, and he and Grandmother wrote an account of a boy who would not fight in battles, and who deserted and ran away with a girl.

The hours, the hidden days, of fear clung to them, long and uncertain as they waited at dusk for the next dawn, Grandfather wrote. But, little by little, the fear of being caught, of death by the sword, receded with the brown, swirling, unfeeling dust outside that was chased in – always chased in – by the wind. Under the damp sacks of rice husks, he held her closer to him, the touch of her salty, soft hair, always reassuring and near. And he saw – could see again – her dry, pale-brown lips through a hazy dream of waking as they found each other alive and warm, only to forever fall again into the depths of cold, mindless fears of sleep, of sleep that was not sleep …

She, Grandmother wrote, took him in her mouth, in fear, reassurance, and fear again, and then an ebbing, quickening, rising, quiver, came from him, before quickly receding again. She gave a cry of sorrow, desolation, of lonely pain as she pushed herself deeper between his feverish thighs, even lower, under the coarse sack, and closed in on him, to assure, to hold on to, to reassure, to revive him, to hold him, never to let go, as he suddenly shivered, moved. As she received him, he flowed, pulling her to him, when in a sudden stupor of blinding despair, Grandfather wrote, he saw the dust break through the cracks in the floorboards above, which creaked with heavy footsteps that tapped, paused, tapped, paused, and tapped again.

His delirium came and went, and as she clung to him and held his weakly tightening, living hands, and finally slept, the barks of dogs receded in the distance, chased by the searching, unseen, unkind, wind.

And, many years later, forgotten by all as they travelled, then hid and travelled again, very far away, and hid again, they were a pair, undisturbed in the vast land, in a new village that did not know them from before, that did not cause them to fear for their lives because they had to fight wars for another, but only gave them the opportunity to grow rice and domesticate animals and raise children.

And, whenever she clung to him on cold winter nights, no longer under floorboards with their shimmering dust in the cruel sunlight, but under a warm quilt, Grandmother wrote, in her tears and cries of receiving him in her, again and again, she never forgot, would never forget, how, in her

Yong Hon Loon
杨 汉 伦

desolate loneliness and despair, she had him for the first time in her mouth, to hold on to him, almost expiring, to reassure herself in her cries of sorrow, that he would shiver, just shiver, show the slightest movement, quiver, flow to her, so she could keep him warm and close, revive him, wake him, never to let him go again.

12

A nd as the one with the white eyebrows and eyelashes, but black hair, wiped his salty white eyelashes with a very tattered handkerchief, he looked up without looking at his would-be executioners; but nothing mattered except what came from his mouth for which he would owe his only life, so he continued his account. But, Grandfather wrote, if anyone were to look closely, which none ever would, as it – or he – did not matter, he was wiping the saltiness that came from looking down deep into himself and not up from under his ever-white eyelashes at his would-be executioners who, in actual fact, meant nothing to him.

As if the famine and the floods that wiped out the people with the great anger of disturbed dragons were not enough, he continued, and as if the killings, attacks, robberies, capture of women, and wars of the rulers, greater or smaller, singly or together, were not enough, there came upon the people in Sugar Mountain the greatest burden to be brought on by the mightiest and angriest dragon.

And this was the dragon that, of all creatures, they had created in their legends in the first place, for the dragon, since it lived in and with them, was from the people who had fair, slightly yellow skin, unique in this land. Since they came together to speak their pre-language, and since they developed a written language, the dragon was in their words, expressions, and writings that held their dreams, legends, tales, stories, divinations – their hopes, desires, pain, joys, and sorrows. It was always alongside them, theirs in all their legacies for all time.

Then the strong rulers among the rulers who had become stronger came to see that it was the dragon which was always alongside the people in times of famine, in times of flood, in times of bountiful harvests of rice. Indeed, it could be theirs alone. And, when they turned their heads, it was the yellow dragon who turned.

13

At this point, his would-be executioners immediately looked at him, Grandfather wrote, for they knew dragons never did, never could, exist; there could never be such imaginary things as dragons. And, as he had no doubt at all that his only head could easily be cut off and no longer be around to forever regret taking the blame for it itself, he continued his account, taking on a more sombre, quieter, and humbler voice.

Every standing stone of the wall not taken away or worn down, he continued, every block, every chip, every mark – pushed, hewn, hammered – every unevenness, evenness, every angled lay or mislay, every wrong made right, every dislodge, every repair, every discovery, every covering could be traced to a pair of hands. There were original pairs, long gone, and then pairs that followed, long gone as well. But that did not mean that no trace of these hands existed, even though no records existed at all to identify the original pair, or, downward through time, the other pairs. This did not mean they had not been there, had not lived or died. But to whomever, wherever, and whenever the link was traced, upwards, there was only a pair. And it had held the stone, the block, the chip.

The pair of hands had fair, slightly yellow skin – hands that were small, or delicate, or strong and muscular. And the links, even though no records existed at all, could be traced through the harshness of the land, its high mountains, barren wastes, freezing blizzards, cruel winters, desolate deserts, hot summers to the greatest burden ever to have befallen Sugar Mountain as it covered the vastness of the vast land. And the links could be traced, upwards, through separation, pain, old age, youthfulness, crushes, falls, frozen deaths, accidents, weaknesses, hunger, diseases, miscarriages, sorrows, and, as always, ultimately, deaths to small, not-so-small, and muscular pairs. Thus*, it came about that …*

The wall, taking away what was worn, torn down, or taken away, was the greatest standing structure in Sugar Mountain that held the greatest number of links that existed in the land, where no records, past or present, existed, to identify the pairs of hands that had built it against the harshness of the land, its high mountains, barren wastes, freezing blizzards, cruel winters, desolate deserts, hot summers. It was built in spite of separations, pain, old age, youthfulness, crushes, falls, frozen deaths, accidents, weaknesses, hunger, diseases, miscarriages, sorrows and, ultimately, deaths. And, with the wall itself, the link, although no memory or remembrance existed at all, to each unique pair – nameless, enduring, forbearing, resigned, accepting – that carried that burden, stone by stone, chip by chip, up the great standing mountains of Sugar Mountain, was unbroken.

14

When it is built piece by piece, no matter for how long or how far across high mountains, its ends will meet. Therefore let these arms embrace you across all time, no matter how far away; then no wall built, no matter how long or how far away, will divide us across high mountains.

—An old reminiscence

Grandfather, who must be with Grandmother, who shared his warmth under the quilt on a cold winter night with the wind howling outside, paused and wrote with Grandmother an account of a man and a woman who died building a wall.

He fell asleep, Grandfather wrote, on the shapeless, incongruous, hard bed of smashed, shattered, frozen shards and stones, her limp, lifeless body beside him. And he drifted into a dream of unspeakable sorrow, entwined with her, holding her to him. As his arm slowly moved, it rubbed against her frozen thighs exposed at the holes in her stiff, padded tunic, torn as they ran, crawled, climbed. He had carried her up the great mountain slopes to escape the fate that was not theirs, that was never meant to be theirs. His heart woke and broke at the sight of her, shrivelled, small, unmoving, her legs buried deep in the soft snow. He touched her with his other unbroken hand, her hair now hard in clumps of ice, and her tightly shut eyes. He wiped, swept, and brushed the snow that was everywhere on her, on him, falling onto her as if it would wake her, open her eyes. But the cold had reached deep and had extinguished her surrendering body, and a howling sadness, sinking, heavy, came to him, into his own depth of cold. He uttered a cry to himself of sorrow and helplessness to see no movement, no tear, but only her unchanged, unmoving, pale, white dimpled cheeks. And as he tried to arch himself to reach beneath her tunic to lift her, pull her, to turn and pull her up, he felt above him a breaking, wailing rumbling from far beyond approaching, echoing everywhere down the great mountain peaks. It was the full fury of an awakening spirit, lunging, tumbling, covering, ripping them down, far down into the voiceless chasm of an unfulfilled, final sleep of forgetfulness, from untold sadness, misery, and pain.

Then, in this dream of unspeakable sorrow, Grandmother wrote, as she fell, still falling, never to leave him, into this dream from which they would not wake, there he was at the spring festival at her door, casting the shadow that never left her heart. And, as she covered him with her padded quilt, to warm him with her joy in seeing him again, of touching his face chilled and kissed by the spring wind, the smell of the distant, yellow hills came to her – new, fresh … the warm breath that belonged to her alone. Then, as he held her closer, warmer, she opening, receiving, and he giving, she gave out a gasp, a laugh, a cry, shrill as a child's, a call to him that only he could hear, moving, searching for her, then finding her, filling her, till, in a surprise that belonged only to them, she closed her eyes, never to open them again, and saw him lying on the dry, rustling grass with her. They rolled in each other's arm, rolling down over fallen spring flowers, finally leaving the distant yellow hills behind over the edge of the ravine into mindless oblivion and nothingness.

15

The one with the white eyebrows and eyelashes, but black hair, Grandfather wrote, wiped his eyelashes – this time with a reason – with his very tattered handkerchief and looked again from the corner of his eye at his would-be executioners, but they did not look at him. It did not mean he did not need to continue, so he continued.

The people with their fair, slightly yellow skin, he continued, who grew rice, spoke, told legends of their dragon, had their language, and made paper, which was common as grass – or themselves – also began to weave silk, which they made into their finest clothes, and – like paper – also wrote and painted on with their ink brushes. But they saw that paper and silk burnt easily and could not be kept forever.

For they who wished to hold on to and keep their possessions for a little longer time also wished for some indestructibility so their legacies would be safe for posterity. They sought permanence, or perpetuity. So they wrote and painted not only on paper and silk, but also on porcelain, which they made only in Sugar Mountain from the soil itself of the vast land. Porcelain became common as paper; they also used it to eat and drink from. Thus *it came about that...*

As they searched for this permanence, as enduring as the dragon of their legends, the supreme rulers, who had conquered other rulers with their large armies of loyal, strong, threatening, and dominant men, thought of what would happen to themselves. Would it be the same as what happened to the people who were as common as grass in the vast land, who had died? For, being the supreme rulers, they should be the ones, rather than the people who were as common as grass, who had the greatest claim to longevity. And the people, who knew in themselves that the supreme rulers in fact came from them, knew how they felt. For when they greeted them, with their heads bowed very low, they never failed – must never fail – in loud voices to call out their wishes for ten thousand years – no, more … tens of thousands years – of life for their supreme rulers. The people knew this was way beyond their mortal lifespan, before they became sentient, even when they started to stand upright. But it was only a wish, a very respectful greeting, to their supreme rulers. And since it met the wishes of the supreme rulers themselves for longevity, the wish, the respectful greeting, came to be used for all rulers and supreme rulers, long into the future.

And those among the people who knew more also knew that, in the eternal life that the supreme rulers wished for, there would be no death, and therefore no birth, and hence the rulers would *not* have been born or come into existence in this vast land at all. And this, of course, was not true – not possible. No, it was totally impossible. It was also insulting and highly disrespectful, for which one deserved to have one's mortal head, even *if* it knew more, or *because* it knew more, cut off. But *it came about that …*

Those among the people who knew more were themselves the ones asked by the supreme rulers to look for the elixir of life.

16

Here the one with the white eyebrows and eyelashes, but black hair, stopped. He thought his would-be executioners moved, even if very slightly, almost imperceptibly. As he wiped his eyelashes yet again – for no reason except to wipe again – with his very tattered handkerchief, his only head, for which he would always be grateful, regained its composure, and he continued in an even more sombre tone, his account.

At this point, Grandfather stopped writing in the old literary tradition in which there were no stops throughout the passage, for although the one with the white eyebrows and eyelashes, but black hair, was still talking, he was resigned to the fact that his head would eventually still be cut off, once he told enough. There was no point in lengthening his tale, even if by a little. Long or short, as it is with all tales, his resigned head then told itself, there would always be an end to the telling, and therefore to itself. Beginnings are beginnings to an end, it reminded itself with

newfound certainty, for which it was very proud, and yet not
happy to have found the certainty. Grandfather continued –
and I wrote from his words – on that winter morning when
Grandmother was still under the familiar old quilt with
him, holding him, quivering, to her.

A few thousand of the boys among the people with fair,
slightly yellow skin, the one with the white eyebrows and
eyelashes, but black hair, continued, and the same number
of girls (for those who knew more knew that the boys, when
they were ready, should not possess more than a girl each
when the girls themselves were ready) were asked to cross
the seas from Sugar Mountain to search for the elixir of life.
For, apart from legends about the vast land itself, there were
legends about the islands across the seas. And one of these
told of people living there in immortality; they, therefore,
must know how to obtain the elixir of life. But, unlike
legends about the vast land itself, which could, if needed, be
easily verified, those about the islands across the seas could
not be. And since they were away from Sugar Mountain, the
only way to verify the legends about the people living there
in a life of immortality was to send those who knew more,
for they should sail there to find out more about the legends.
So *it came about that …*

Those who knew more sailed across the seas with the
thousands of boys and the same number of girls. But those
who knew more already knew – from knowing more – that
there was no elixir of life, and they could not find those
who lived in immortality when they landed on the islands.
The elixir of life could not be obtained if these beings, who
were supposed to be immortal, were not around in the first
place. For, although these islands were away from Sugar

Mountain, they were not very different in most respects, except that they were not at all vast; they were just small islands. But they were away from the vast land, and therefore legends about those who lived there needed to be verified.

Thus, not finding what they went there to find, those who knew more, and the thousands of boys and girls with them, stayed on the islands, which for the first time were being visited by people with fair and slightly yellow skin from the vast land – for a while. After some time, those who knew more – but not the thousands of boys and girls – could not stay any longer and wished to return to their home in Sugar Mountain. But, as they had not found those who lived there in perpetuity, and therefore did not know how to obtain the elixir of life, they would return on pain of having their heads, which knew more, cut off. This was no reason at all for returning. For, if they had known how to find the elixir of life, they could easily partake of it, and even if they had returned with nothing, their heads, which knew more, could never be cut off, for, if they were already immortal, there was nothing to fear even from the supreme rulers who were, up to the time before they left them, still mortal. Thus *it came about that …*

Those who knew more, who could not return to Sugar Mountain without having their heads cut off, still returned without knowing how to obtain the elixir of life. Then many years later, they had again to return to the islands across the seas, since their heads had fortunately not been cut off upon their return to Sugar Mountain, to again find those who lived there who knew how to obtain the elixir of life. Still, of course, those who knew more knew that there was no such thing, having been there before. But they had to return to the islands so that their heads would still not be cut off. And this was their second chance. If they returned again without the elixir of life, their heads would finally be cut off by the supreme rulers, who, having been told once before, would never believe them the second time around. Thus *it came about that ...*

The descendants of the people from Sugar Mountain who had fair, slightly yellow skin, who sailed across the seas for immortality, who were not allowed to return again to the vast land without having their heads cut off, would *never again* return to Sugar Mountain.

17

As the one with the white eyebrows and eyelashes, but black hair, slightly – ever so slightly – turned his only head to his would-be executioners, it seemed to him that they were quite pleased to hear the words *never again*, even though he had earlier thought they were not really listening to what he had to say, which, as it turned out, was not true at all. His only head, thinking to itself, told itself never *ever* to think that way again, or eventually, or sooner than eventually, it would no longer be. Thus he, Grandfather wrote, continued. But with his next breath – it being that soon – he entirely forgot what his only head told him not to do so that it would not find that it would no longer be.

Those who knew more who would travel again, never to return, to the islands across the seas, confirmed that they, like everyone else, did not want to have their heads cut off. Because no one who lived in the islands there knew how to obtain the elixir of life, there was no choice but to look for an alternative. Thus *it came about that* …

Those who knew more, but who were fortunate enough not to be asked to sail across the seas in search of the secret, or secrets, of immortality, were asked to *make*, from what was found in the vast land itself, the elixir of life. But, unlike those who had earlier sailed across the seas, they eventually told the truth – the elixir of life, tested on supreme rulers who, unlike those who usurped or came after them, were unfortunate enough to die, could *not* be made. So there was no elixir, and no supreme rulers who came after lived forever. They, like the people who were as common as grass, with their fair, slightly yellow skin, would die in their time, prematurely or otherwise.

But, being supreme rulers, they still must have a way – as all beginnings must have an end – for them alone to seek the way to immortality, even if immortality itself was confirmed totally beyond reach by all who knew more. Therefore *it came about that* …

Since the men in the vast land, even before they became sentient, could own and possess more than one woman, the supreme rulers, being who they were, should deem that they should be able to possess, unlike the men who were as common as grass, an infinite number of women. For, since their women gave birth, and, in time, their sons who came after them would have children, and their grandsons would have their own children, and so on, for a long line of descendants, the supreme rulers would have obtained some measure, at least, of eternity, even though they were born to die, like all the men and women who were as common as grass. But that did not matter, so long as when they were alive, they knew that they would have these descendants descended from them, which should make them happy when they were dying, or on the verge of dying. This was provided they were given women in some infinite number – as many as they could keep – to ensure nothing untoward happened, as, down through the generations, all who came after would still be mortal. Thus *it came about that …*

The supreme rulers did finally achieve this measure of immortality – for as many women as the rulers or supreme rulers were capable of and manly enough to fulfil, could, and therefore might, ensure the possibility of infinity. This would provide that the links, down through the generations, at any point along the expected very long line to their descendants, would not, for any reason, be broken. Hence *it came about that …*

A practice was devised that was to be found only in the land of Sugar Mountain: Every person – anyone – who was within the reach of the supreme ruler's women in their infinitely possible numbers had to be either a woman or a man who was not a man. These men were no longer men because their manliness had been cut off, so that they could be near the supreme rulers and their infinitely possible number of women. No men who were men – none at all whatsoever except for the supreme rulers themselves – were ever allowed to be near them, as only men who were no longer men could be trusted. In this unique way the supreme rulers alone in Sugar Mountain ensured that measure of immortality for themselves, as they, rightly as supreme rulers, could then be sure that that measure of immortality was theirs, and not others'. And, with this practice, for them there was finally the newfound peace of mind for that measure of eternity, even with their backs turned momentarily, which they knew from experience was always how things happened.

18

What happened next could only be expected, not just by the head of the one with the white eyebrows and eyelashes, but black hair, to which he owed everything. All could see that. His would-be executioners looked at him again, which, especially at this point, after all that had gone before, was not good for it, or him, at all. He, Grandfather wrote, had to make changes, and quickly, for its sake, since it was the only head he had. So he quickly continued his account without pausing in spite of what had already been said. To return to the previous state where his would-be executioners appeared not to be bothered about him by appearing not to look at him, he put away his very tattered handkerchief for good, no longer wiping his eyelashes with it. And what could be better to talk about than the people of Sugar Mountain themselves to encourage his would-be executioners not to look at him again.

The people, he continued, reverting to what he had mentioned earlier to be on the safe side, had, among the many things they had made, paper, which they widely used to wipe themselves after they cleared their bowels. And they used paper, which became as common as grass, common as they, to wipe themselves and their wives, or the women with them, in bed after they fulfilled their desires, if they, in the course of it, soiled themselves or their women. For paper was handy and necessary in their lives; it was made and came to be used everywhere and anywhere – to clean, to wipe, to cover, to wrap. Thus *it came about that …*

After they had a pre-language, and then a language, the people first made inscriptions on animal bones and shells, on pottery made from clay, and on bamboo strips. These were all hard surfaces from which the inscriptions could not be wiped off easily. Neither was it easy to make the inscriptions, which were their first words and numbers – for counting, for naming, for owning what was written on, for divinations for hunts, for good harvests of rice, to keep floods and famine at bay. But paper was not a hard substance. It was easy to write on, and was plentiful. Their words, therefore, came to be written on paper, which was as common as the people who made and used it, that they used to wipe themselves after their bowels moved, and after they and their women fulfilled their desires, and to clean, to wipe, to cover, to wrap in their daily lives. And their divinations, their numbers, their dates, their legends, their tales, their histories could be written on it. It was a common, everyday, plentiful substance, suitable for all and for many purposes. And many could own what was written on paper – divinations, numbers, dates, legends, tales and histories – which could be kept and passed on, unlike what was heard and told, and told and heard, by word of mouth. So *it came about that …*

Yong Hon Loon
杨 汉 伦

The paper that the people made, on which they wrote with brush and ink, could later be printed on and bound into books for recording their writings and for their paintings. And its use quickly spread far and wide in the vast land. And as it became as common as the rice they ate, as common as grass, as common as they themselves, the use of language, and what it was used for, spread – on paper and in books.

19

Here the one with white eyebrows and eyelashes, but black hair, paused. Then, changing his mind, he took out his very tattered handkerchief to wipe his eyelashes, only for the sake of wiping, as if to defy his only head. For what he had next to tell, Grandfather wrote, he had to tell, even if it meant the end to the telling if his would-be executioners turned again to look at him. But, he told his only head, which was alerted to by then – and was alarmed by - his ever-present stubbornness, he would make it short and tell it quickly. So he continued, quickly, to show it.

If the paper made by the people of Sugar Mountain was plentiful, he continued in a single breath, and books bound from it were also plentiful, and if much could be written and printed into books by those who knew more, and if these writings printed into books could spread quickly throughout the vast land, and those who came to have the books read and could keep the books, then books printed from paper were not to be taken lightly if the writings in the books could turn the minds of the people who were as common as grass in the vast land. For those who knew more, who themselves were of the people who had fair, slightly yellow skin, did eventually write as many books as they could. And books, not mortal like all mortal beings high and low, carried what was written in them, which when kept, carried the likelihood in them that they would be passed on down to descendants who could then read about what had happened before and what had been done to the people who were as common as the grass they stepped on, who had come before them.

But paper, though plentiful, also, fortunately, burnt, he added, very quickly. Thus *it came about that …*

Since books, which were plentiful, were not to be taken lightly when they could turn the people's minds, they were burnt throughout the vast land when they were seen to be able to turn the people's minds. It was the greatest burning of books and paper – made by the people themselves in the vast land – that ever raged throughout Sugar Mountain.

However, although the books were burnt in the greatest burning that ever happened in the land, the many who had written the books were still around. And they could, if they would, still write or re-write, and their writings could again be printed into books, which, since paper was plentiful, as common as the people in the land, as common as grass, could again also be plentiful. Thus *it came about that …*

Those who knew more and wrote books that were seen to be able to turn the people's minds were also buried with their books so that they could no longer write or re-write the books that had been burnt or buried with them. And it was the greatest burial of all who knew more who wrote books. He quickly ended his story, which satisfied himself but, more critically, hopefully did not make his would-be executioners flinch or turn their heads, even if it was only slightly, short as the account might be.

20

In the approaching darkness of the receding horizon,
only let me be buried in your arms; let the red glow
of your cheeks and warmth of your lips calling out
to me, searching in the valleys for me, warm and
shelter me in this cold merciless pit of endless silence
from which I will not return.

—An old reminiscence

Grandfather, who could be with Grandmother, who
held him close not to let him go, paused and, with
Grandmother, wrote an account of a man who wrote books
who was buried because he wrote the books he wrote.

He was arraigned with the rest, Grandfather wrote, near
a corner where there were ladders that went down into pits.
Sacks of soil were tied to the legs of the ladders so that they
did not sink into the newly dug soil under the weight of the

men like him who climbed up and down to dig the pits, carrying their full basket loads of soil on their backs – the same soil which, after the pits were dug, would be thrown back to bury those who dug it up.

The summer sun and air above were hot and shimmering, but it was hotter and damp inside the deepening pits where the heat mixed the smell of the soil with the smell of their sweat, as their bodies rubbed, smooth, sticky, warm, and alive, against each other as they continued to dig. They were silent, none talking to another, which was unusual for men who wrote, but not unusual for those faced with this situation.

When the pit was dug to a sufficient depth, he suspected, talking to himself in the calm of one facing a known outcome, the ladders, but not the men, would be hauled up. He laughed without laughing. It was to be soon. The faster they dug, and the harder they worked, the sooner it was to be. The rough shovel caused blisters on both his hands, but to him the pain was far away, where she was. He remembered his dog had been poisoned the night before; but he had already told her to go to her village home, with her belongings, on a donkey. And as the blisters tore and his skin started to bleed, the smell of her breath, of her hair, and the warmth of her clear, white breasts, her thighs and fine calves – all of this came back and warmed him, as he bent under the weight of a great tiredness, greater than any that he had ever known before. He stood in his thin hemp tunic trousers as the soil all around went into his mouth, nose and eyes.

She knew, Grandmother wrote, that he would not return. The night before – it was always at night – they had come up to his home across the red hills, to go through his books, which they pushed and crammed into their sacks, as if they would be reading them all, as if they understood all that was written and was yet to be written. The rest that did not fit into the sacks they stepped on ferociously as if by doing so what was written in the books would then no longer matter, for not all books which were written could be found and burnt in the vast land.

She knew, under his familiar old quilt, as she pushed her head closer, under his chin. And she needed to hear the beats coming from him, to hold his warmth to her – but there were only desperation, impossible hopes, and unreachable outcomes, beyond seeking, far as the distant cries of ospreys in the dark, desolate, and unforgiving night. And as he held her even closer to him, she did not, would not, let him go, as the engulfing swirl of all uncertainties, except the one certainty – his end – kept them away from all that was around them except themselves.

And as they, from way above, away from them, threw the newly dug soil back into the pits with them finally inside, Grandfather wrote, he could no longer stand, but lay down with the earth against his cheeks, to feel her feet running to him on the damp moss in the mist that flowed in spring from the valley of plum blossoms far from the red hills of their homes.

21

And the one with white eyebrows and eyelashes, but black hair, after telling what he had then to tell – and quickly – next whispered what he still needed to whisper. He was just within earshot of his would-be executioners, and he hoped that they would not be hearing too much – that they would not be alerted to turn their heads – since he had already quickened his telling. So he continued by whispering what he had to whisper. Thus *it came about that* …

The greatest burning of books in Sugar Mountain occurred, and this was done so that there would be no memory of the books burnt, and no present-day mind could discover, without any evidence whatsoever handed down through time, what had been done to the books of those who knew more, and also to the people of the vast land. But having no memory of the books did not mean no trace of them existed. The reason for their being and the cause of their destruction could still be traced down through the generations. However, everything that had been written by those who knew more in all the books that were burnt was lost for all time, and the links to the books and what was written in them – not lost through time – were, in their burning, irretrievably broken.

In the greatest burial to occur in the vast land, the links traced to the beings who wrote the books – the authors – were, at the same time, broken. But the reason for their burial – the cause of their ends – could still be traced down so that the present-day mind could see and understand this link to the past of long ago. But for all who were buried there for writing their books, the links to all further generations from them were also irretrievably broken, and never present.

22

The one with white eyebrows and eyelashes, but black hair, after what he had said about the greatest burning and burial in Sugar Mountain, dared not look at his would-be executioners; neither did he dare to wipe his eyelashes, particularly just for the sake of wiping, with his very tattered handkerchief. For, Grandfather wrote, it could really lead to the end. But he knew, and his only head knew, that his would-be executioners knew that it could not be, for the greatest burning and burial had taken care of matters, and therefore there was more to come. So he continued without looking and without wiping, which, in the first place, he should not have started at all. He should have started nothing at all that would alert or alarm his would-be executioners.

With the elixir of life not found, he continued, the supreme rulers, with their loyal, strong, threatening, and dominant men, could continue in their battles and wars against each other for a long time. And each time a struggle among them was won, those who won, knowing that they were not immortal, would see to it that those they had won over, along with their wives, their children, their children's children, and so on, were killed, in their entirety, so that they could not return in some future time to defeat them in battles and wars. In this way, even though they were not immortal, the winning supreme rulers had assured the perpetuity of the fact that those they defeated would not return for all time to defeat them ever again, as the link to further generations had been broken.

And so this continued for a long time in Sugar Mountain. And *it came about that …*

There were those among those who knew more who *said* that they knew more. And these who said they knew more wrote books for the people so that all would know who among them should be above others, and who among those above others should be above them, and who, in turn, upwards, should be above those, and so on. Since, after the people stood upright, and had fair, slightly yellow skin, the men had owned and possessed their women, right as roosters were among hens, husbands were above wives. And, in turn, the older, who, like those who said they knew more, knew more because they were older, were above the young. So it went on, according to the books they wrote, which were not burnt, until everyone in the vast land knew who was above whom and whom to obey. Everyone knew his or her place without doubt, all the way up to the supreme rulers, who were above all, or, at least, all who, at any given time, were below them. For the supreme rulers, at any given time, unlike everyone else in the vast land for which the books were written, could not agree among themselves who among them was above whom. And they had to fight battles and wars to find out. But the battles and wars that should settle this for good often could not settle this, and so the wars continued for a long time. This notwithstanding, the supreme rulers fighting among themselves had this in common – they would not destroy the books written for everyone else by those who said they knew more, as all were below them, whose heads were therefore never at risk of being cut off. Thus *it came about that* …

After they who said they knew more wrote their books, and the books were read by the people in the land, everyone knew who was above whom, with no quibble and no doubt. So far a long time – a very long time since there was remembrance and books written of it – in the vast land of Sugar Mountain, within the very long wall, where the people with their fair, slightly yellow skin, who spoke, had a language, told legends of their dragon, made paper, silk and porcelain – the people listened to what was written, which was not burnt, and which everyone read, understood, and followed. And for a long time they made nothing at all. For the wall, built by many who died building it a long time ago, to keep others out, kept them in.

But, using the same lodestone that they had made for use very much earlier, just as they had made paper, and with the help of maps, which they could make for travel across wide, unforgiving oceans, others outside of the wall who did not have the fair, slightly yellow skin, but had fairer skin, and who came from far away, came and saw what they in Sugar Mountain made and could make, and *they* changed and went on to make what the people in the vast land did not, could not, or would not make. So those who came from afar changed, as the people in Sugar Mountain, who believed those who said they knew more, did not change.

23

Not a bowl of sour rice wine or a tattered book of poems; only a glimpse of your white thighs, your smooth calves, and your small feet to sooth my sleep on this hard, unfeeling winter bed.

—An old reminiscence

The one with the white eyebrows and eyelashes, but black hair, Grandfather wrote, stole a look at his would-be executioners and, certain that all was as before, or before the before – he could not remember … at least the before that was to the advantage of his only head – he continued his account with a slightly, almost imperceptibly, different air. It could even be a happier air which, given his predicament – his only head shook to itself, having little or no faith in him – was incongruous, ridiculous, almost stupid.

The people, both men and women, he continued, finally
found in foot binding – a practice that had to begin early
in childhood to be successful, but only among women –
a popular and widespread custom, a convergence of their
mutual desires, both the men's and the women's. It was not
enough that the women of the vast land had fair, slightly
yellow skin, round breasts, and full thighs, and hair in
their groins and armpits, which they were born with, and
appealed to the men. The custom of foot binding – even as
the people made nothing new for a long time – became a
new, common standard to measure women by, both by the
men who desired them, and by the women who looked at
themselves, at their feet. Thus *it came about that* ...

The practice, with its distortion, deformity, pain, and
discomfort for the rest of the women's lives, had to be done
right at childhood to prevent any further growth of the feet.
But this distortion, deformity, pain, and discomfort happened
not to be borne by the men, who were above their women.
As they desired their women, and as the women wished
to be desired in turn, they finally found, in the women's
greater awkwardness, difficulty, contortion, vulnerability,
and helplessness below the men, a novel physical, and an
even more heightened differentiation of men from women,
of women with bound feet and those without. Foot binding
resulted in a bodily suppression, slowness, weakness, and
renewed dependency, which was what was wanted by the
men, and therefore by their women. Their past desires,
perceptions, dreams and longings for the women – just as
they fought over them in the gatherings when they started to
walk upright and were sentient – were now new and greater,
which provided them greater excitement, which also made

the women happier. And the practice was accepted by many in the vast land and quickly spread. So *it came about that …*

The practice, which, like many things women, started primarily with the supreme rulers' women, who always took the best care of themselves and were the best adorned in the land, soon became ubiquitous as all took up the practice. It was, and became, the means to show, to elevate themselves, to walk with the same awkwardness, which might even be regarded as grace or gracefulness, even though they were not rulers' women. It was a differentiation and attraction that they who wished to be desired by the men, though they were not rulers' women, could not let pass.

Thus this unique and novel practice found nowhere else but in the vast land of Sugar Mountain became a happy convergence of what the men, who desired their women, and women, in their wish for greater elevation and attraction to the men who desired them, wanted. So the women, whose ancestors started to stand upright, which differentiated them from animals, now still walked upright but with bound feet, with a new awkwardness, helplessness, vulnerability, even grace or gracefulness, which still differentiated them from animals that did not walk upright, but now further differentiated them from men, under whom they already were, and also from other women with lesser attraction for men – those who did not have bound feet, and therefore no grace or gracefulness, or elevation from commonness, from people common as grass, although they were people common as grass, and not the rulers' women.

And, as it continued to be favoured, down through the generations, by those who came after, the novel custom, unique to the vast land, continued for a long time in Sugar Mountain, where nothing new was made, or was still made.

24

She appeared, still in her embroidered narcissus-white wedding gown, as a ghost; but it was the most beautiful ghost ever encountered with the living.

—An old reminiscence

Grandfather, who could be in bed with Grandmother with her arms round him, paused, and both she and Grandfather wrote an account of a poor, young girl whose mother bound her feet when she was very young, who was betrothed as a younger wife of many wives to a man she had never met, to live at a place she had never known in her young life.

As she stood with her bound feet perched, shaking, at the edge of the high waterfall, Grandmother wrote, she heard again the loud roars of languid but rudely awakened dragons that beckoned her out of her forlorn, lonely tears of sleepless dreams, to wet, billowing mists of rainbow bridges that would carry her across to new sunshine. It would carry her away – far away – from the all the reds of the sedan chair, of embroidered shoes, of the veil, of the scrolls hanging down the walls, of the bridal chamber, of the poster bed, of the sticky crimson red of the ever-flowing pain that came from her, ruptured, shamed, under the red embroidered quilt in which she hid herself, from herself, shrivelled, naked, small, even smaller under the ox thrusts, heavy, drunken, panting, spitting, biting … the cruel impatience, the sweatiness, the throwing, the plunging, the tearing of her red padded blouse until, finally, among the reds of the quilt, blanket, veil, padded gown, the sticky crimson red flowing down her legs covered her in shame, in her nakedness, in sobbing, forlorn, lonely tears that he, far away, very far away, could not hear.

Far away, Grandfather wrote, from pre-arrangements, arrangements, betrothals, ownership, possession, dependency, contortion, awkwardness, pain, cruelty, shame.

Then, as she fell, Grandmother continued, she closed her eyes to the beckoning dragons, roaring, carrying her across onto the rainbow bridges, her torn red padded blouse drifting, fluttering, floating far, very far, away from her as she went down, beyond, swallowed in the depths of his rippling laughter into his receiving arms waiting for her to join him, to hold him, to keep him from the very far away.

25

In the midst of the account of the one with white eyebrows and eyelashes, but black hair, Grandfather wrote, his only head, to which he owed the debt of his mortal life, suddenly gave him a rude nudge. For his would-be executioners, who already had spent a very long day with nothing to show for it, were showing signs – even the slightest, unseen signs – of impatience. And this was not good for his only head. So he thought hard, and eventually seeing what his only head wanted, made a jump in his account to prevent anything happening to it at this late stage.

The people in the vast land, he said, resuming his story, continued to live their lives. They grew rice, desired their women, and, where they could avoid it, left their supreme rulers to fight among themselves. And they continued to follow what had been written by those who said they knew more. For *it came about that* …

The people in the vast land, who were around for quite some time, would still be around for quite some time. For those who said they knew more told the people, in the books they wrote, that they should have a thousand sons and ten thousand grandsons. And, as the people believed in them, they tried not to disappoint them whenever they were with the women they desired. But, a thousand sons and ten thousand grandsons appeared to hint at – even if it was the merest hint – granting the people who were as common as grass, as common as the paper they made, with a little, a very tiny, measure of immortality. Given their commonness, a thousand and ten thousand were outcomes that were infinitely improbable for all who were common. Those who said they knew more knew this, for what they wrote in their books, which was read by the people, was about a thousand sons and ten thousand grandsons, their numbers. Thus *it came about that* ...

The numbers of sons and grandsons grew greatly in the vast land, which was what those who said they knew more had foreseen. But it did not provide even a little – even the tiniest measure – of immortality to anyone as common as grass, as common as paper. It provided the supreme rulers with more loyal, strong, threatening, and dominant sons and grandsons of the people to fight their battles and wars, and, because they were loyal, to die for them, to be replaced, in turn, by other sons and grandsons. This ensured they remained supreme rulers, even if not in perpetuity, for that much longer.

26

After the one with the white eyebrows and eyelashes, but black hair, made a jump in his long account for the sake of his only head, and for himself, without any untoward consequence, Grandfather wrote, he found, from another rude nudge from his only head, which was not smart, as it made him flinch, which could alert his would-be executioners, that he had no choice. At this point he must make a jump, as did the people of Sugar Mountain, who had made nothing for a long time. There were people from far away who could, for the first time, really come through their wall in spite of the wall. But this also meant that he, together with his only head, would be near their ends.

Many of the people from far away, who did not have fair, slightly yellow skin, but had fairer skin, he continued, definitely for the last time, came to Sugar Mountain. *It came about that …*

They came because it was a vast land and, together with what was in the land, the ancestors of the people with their fair, slightly yellow skin, had what they made, which was only found in the vast land and nowhere else. And, together with those who came from far away, many of those from across the seas, who also had fair, slightly yellow skin – a very long time after those who had sailed across the seas and could not return to the vast land – came to the vast land because it was, or in spite of the fact that it was, a vast land.

With those from far away, together with those from across the seas, coming to the land, those in the vast land had little or no choice; they could – where they could – ensure the situation was not changed, or was not changed too much, to see to their own position. Or, if the situation was not to their advantage, they could – where they could – pacify those from far away or across the seas, to still see to their own position, which should then not change to their disadvantage. And, if the situation was worse, or was worsening, or, more disturbing, was very worrying, which was totally not to their advantage at all, they could – where they could – get those who came from far away or across the seas to be on their side, or, more accurately, be on the side of those many who came through to the vast land.

27

As he spoke, at this point, the one with white eyebrows and eyelashes, but black hair, suddenly stopped, Grandfather wrote, for a hard blow, coming from out of nowhere, landed on his only head, which made him fall very hard backwards. Staggering, and awkwardly regaining his composure from this sudden bolt of a blow, he continued, but very differently from what he last spoke about, for the sake of both his only head and himself. *It came about that ...*

He said in the same voice that had carried him to where he still was – surprisingly not reeling, not sore, unworried, unaffected in his telling by the hard hit on his head – so long as it allowed him to tell what he had finally to tell, no matter what happened to himself and his head. Even if it meant the end to them, the telling could not, must not, end. When those who came from far away, and those who came from across the seas came to Sugar Mountain, they found not a man – as was written and foretold by those who said they knew more – but a woman who was supposed to be one among the infinitely possible number of women to ensure that measure of immortality for a man. Those who said they knew more, in spite of knowing more and in spite of the people believing in them, totally had not foreseen all this in their writings and in their many books that, in the death of a rooster among hens, there would be a hen no rooster was mounting. A hen who could rid herself of roosters if she wanted, whither the land.

And, contrary to what those who said they knew more foresaw and wrote in their books, no rooster was forthcoming, or would ever be forthcoming, as the hen would not and could not be mounted by roosters. It was a hen, it turned out, no rooster could mount, since there were no men but only those who were no longer men, all having had their manliness cut off. As it turned out, this had been done totally in vain to ensure that measure of immortality for a man no longer around.

And those who had come from far away could see that this was advantageous to them. Closer still, those who had come from across the seas, who also had fair, slightly yellow skin, who a very long time ago were not allowed to return without having their heads cut off, could also see that. And they could see that they could return this time with no fear whatsoever of having their heads cut off, which was very advantageous to them. For, let alone having no fear for their heads, they had no fear even of those who came from far away, from whom they were able, after those from far away made them, to make what they were able to make. Therefore, they could come across the seas to Sugar Mountain, in spite of it being a vast land, with no fear at all. Thus *it came about that …*

As there was no man with any measure of immortality in the vast land, but a woman, the people witnessed for the first time, unleashed upon Sugar Mountain from outside its wall, built a long time ago by the many who died building it in order to prevent what they feared would happen in the future time, which had finally come about, what was far greater than all that was ever unleashed upon it by the dragons of its legends in perennial floods and famines, and by the battles and wars fought by its supreme rulers. And the bamboo, then not in bloom, that always bent but never broke, was bent to be broken.

As he ended his account, Grandfather and Grandmother finally wrote together, her hand, by then quivering, close, very close and warm in his, each word in his round, bold, and soft brush stroke followed by one in her fine, thin, and delicate stroke, until, at the end, they combined their brush strokes in each word to form new, unique strokes. A tear came under the white eyelashes of the one with white eyebrows and black hair, which his would-be executioners saw. They were visibly moved for the first time without any doubt whatsoever, which was definitely to the advantage of his only head to which, never in doubt, he truly owed his life. And, for the first time, his would-be executioners saw that, under his ever-white eyelashes, he who had spoken so long in order not to have his only head cut off at the end, unlike them, could not see.

28

His account ended, and his only life spared, the one with the white eyebrows and eyelashes, but black hair, in spite of his age, finally walked out to the white, fresh fallen snow, outside to the vast land that he always carried in him, had in him, and lived in him. He breathed it in as if for the very first time, still talking out loud, but now to himself, and no longer in that sombre voice. And those outside in the snow who heard him, as he turned his head, saw that he had white eyebrows and eyelashes, but black hair, so they left him alone.

In an ending without ending, or a would-be ending that was no ending, he continued, now without his would-be executioners, who finally had something to show for their efforts, there would be a new telling, a re-telling, a surprise morning – a new beginning. For, it was an undeniable fact, a given, that we did not choose all who preceded us – our ancestors. They chose us. This is a given, or truth, that we always need to remember, to recall, to remind ourselves of.

Sugar Mountain and the Descendants of a Man
and a Woman Who Died Building a Wall

We ourselves are proof that they once existed. Without them we would not be, and, he then concluded with a voice full of the joy and sunshine of the surprise morning, because of what they were, and what they had become, we would be.

29

In the end, as I took out the last piece of writing from Grandmother and Grandfather's camphor wood chest, with its familiar scent from the old tree from which it came, it looked for the first time since I was with and then without Grandmother, empty – *quiet.*

In it, Grandmother, in her thin, delicate but this time uneven brush strokes, the first without Grandfather's, wrote for the last time on the day of the surprise morning they met, which was also the day she left Grandfather. As I read it, I knew she knew. She had given me Grandfather's eyes, and his name and, with it, the fragile link unbroken in her, the predisposed outcome. With the many that stood to confront what was unleashed, Grandfather paid with himself – but not Grandmother.

She wrote in her final letter to me – to Grandfather she finally returned to:

> *In the end* (Grandfather's name which was mine) *did not leave.* (Our name) *wanted me to go without waiting for any longer time, so that* (our name) *was sure the joy we have together, our only joy, left with me, very far away. I left* (our name) *in the sunshine of the surprise morning – this morning – when we met. When the days close for me to cross the night sky, I will sleep again under the mulberry trees and willows in spring to be with you, my* (our name).

For me, who could not bear but to destroy all their writings in their fine, thin, delicate, round, bold and soft brush strokes, dedicated only to each other, it was the end of a promise I made to myself in Grandfather's name, which I kept. And I knew, at that time, that Grandmother – with no other known relation in the world – knew. And knew that it would be kept.

Printed in the United States
By Bookmasters